Nothing But A Pig

WRITTEN AND ILLUSTRATED BY
BROCK COLE

Doubleday & Company, Inc., Garden City, New York

ISBN: 0-385-17063-7 Trade
ISBN: 0-385-17064-5 Prebound
Library of Congress Catalog Card Number 80-8643
Text & Illustrations copyright © 1981 by Brock Cole

To Rachel

Once there was a poor man who had a pig he would not sell.
  "It would be like selling a friend," he said to his wife. "Would you
have me sell my friend?"

Of course his wife would not, and they managed as best they could on the money they earned selling fresh vegetables and eggs.

"They are not my friends," the poor man explained.

His name was Avril, his wife was Agnes, and his pig was named Preston.

In the evening after work Avril would take his pipe to the pigpen. There he would sit down and tell Preston about the events of his day. Preston was a good listener and enjoyed Avril's stories of village life.

But misunderstandings can occur between even the best of friends.

The truth is that Avril spoiled Preston. After a while, the pig began to think that he was finer than his poor friend.
   "I was meant for better things," thought Preston.
   "He thinks he is too good for the likes of me," thought Avril. "If he is not careful, I will sell him."

One day a rich man named Grabble, who owned the tiny cottage where Avril and Agnes lived, came to collect the yearly rent.

"The rent is doubled this year," said Mr. Grabble.

He had heard of Avril's fine pig, and wanted him for himself. He was very fond of bacon and ham.

"Then I cannot pay," said Avril.

"Then I shall have your pig," said Mr. Grabble.

"Well, why not? " thought Avril to himself. "He is, after all, nothing but a pig."

So he took Mr. Grabble to the pigpen.

PIG NOT for SALE

When Preston saw the rich Mr. Grabble approaching, something stirred in his soul.

Mr. Grabble's shoes were shining. His suit fitted perfectly over his round stomach. His hair was combed neatly over the bald spot in the middle of his head, and he waved the flies away with a handkerchief that smelled of roses.

"Now there is a man I could admire," thought Preston.

"He'll do," said Mr. Grabble.

Mr. Grabble tied a rope to Preston's neck and led him away to his fine house in the village.

In the back of the Grabble house was a garden filled with flowers. At the end of the garden was a small pen, hidden by a bower of roses. There Mr. Grabble left Preston.

"What a fine house!" thought Preston. "What fine gardens!" He nibbled delicately at a spray of roses that hung over his pen.

Secretly he was disappointed that Mr. Grabble had not taken him into his house and introduced him to the family.

The truth struck him suddenly.

"I am not presentable! I need a bath, and"—he blushed pink with shame—"I have nothing to wear."

After a moment's thought, he unlatched the gate to his pen and walked to the back door of the house.

No one was in the kitchen. Preston refreshed himself with two cabbages and a bunch of carrots that had been left on the scrubbed table.

No one was in the hall . . .

or on the stairs . . .

or in the master bathroom.

Preston drew a bath and scrubbed himself thoroughly with
Mr. Grabble's scented pink soap.

No one was in the dressing room where Mr. Grabble kept his fine clothes. They fitted Preston admirably. In one of the pockets he found a pocketbook filled with money.

"How thoughtful of Mr. Grabble," said Preston to himself, "to see that I have everything that I need."

When the servant girl glanced into the parlor, she was startled.

"That must be Mr. Grabble's uncle, come to visit a day early, and no one to welcome him," she thought. She went into the parlor, curtsied low, and announced that Mr. Grabble had gone to his office at the bank, but that Mrs. Grabble would be back soon. She asked Preston if he would care for coffee and cake while he waited.

"Snort! Snuffle, gruff," said Preston politely.

"How gruff he is. I can barely understand him," thought the servant girl, "but his eyes are kind."

Away she went to fetch the coffee and cake.

At three o'clock Mrs. Grabble returned. She could hear someone playing the harmonium in the front parlor.

"It's Mr. Grabble's uncle, ma'am, come a day early," said the servant girl.

"Goodness!" said Mrs. Grabble, and went in to greet her husband's uncle.

"How stout he has grown," she thought.

"How well you look," she said.

She explained that they had not expected him so soon, and that Mr. Grabble had gone to the bank. Preston excused himself and went off to the bank to meet Mr. Grabble.

When he was gone, Mrs. Grabble went out into the garden to see the new pig. When she saw that the pig was gone and the gate was unlatched, she was very disturbed. She went back to the house to telephone her husband.

The servant girl met her at the door. She was very excited.

"A robber has taken Mr. Grabble's best suit, two cabbages, a bunch of carrots, and a bath," she said.

Mrs. Grabble said, "We must be calm. He has taken a pig as well. We can only be thankful that Mr. Grabble's uncle was not disturbed."

While the servant girl fixed her a cup of tea with four lumps of sugar, Mrs. Grabble telephoned her husband and told him what had happened.

He was very annoyed. It made him feel only a little better to learn that his uncle had arrived a day early and was coming to his office to meet him.

In the meantime, Avril had begun to regret that he had given Preston to Mr. Grabble to be made into bacon and ham.

"My best friend," he said to his wife. "How could I have paid our rent with my best friend? I must have been insane."

He left for the bank immediately, determined to bring Preston back at any cost.

When he reached the bank and was shown into Mr. Grabble's office, he barely noticed the fine, portly gentleman standing by the window.

"Mr. Grabble," he began, "I made a terrible mistake this morning when I let you take my pig away. He is my best friend."

Preston (for, of course, Preston was the gentleman by the window) was deeply touched.

"Such devotion," he thought, "I had no idea."

Mr. Grabble, however, became angrier than ever. Since he no longer had Avril's pig, he decided to pretend that he had never had it.

"Pig? What pig? I don't have your dirty pig, and you owe me one year's rent," he shouted.

Preston was hurt and shocked by these words.

"The man is a cad," he thought. He realized that he had been deceived by appearances.

Making up his mind instantly, Preston thrust his loaded purse into Avril's hands. The amount of money in the purse was exactly what Avril owed.

"Here is the rent," said Avril wonderingly.

"Sniffle, snort!" added Preston indignantly, and threw off Mr. Grabble's suit. He had learned that fine clothes do not make a man.

Avril was surprised that Preston was in the banker's office, but glad to have his friend back. Preston was sorry that he had considered leaving his friend even for a moment.

They went back to Avril's house together, where Agnes was waiting for them. That night they had a lovely supper of corn and turnips. It was delicious.